The Penguin Problem

by ABBY KLEIN

illustrated by
JOHN McKINLEY

Scholastic Inc.

New York Toronto London Auckland
Sydney Mexico City New Delhi Hong Kong

To Jules, Brody, Jonah, and Oliver,
I love you all!
Love,
A. K.

No part of this publication may be reproduced, stored in a retrieval system, or transmitted in any form or by any means, electronic, mechanical, photocopying, recording, or otherwise, without written permission of the publisher. For information regarding permission, write to Scholastic Inc., Attention: Permissions Department, 557 Broadway, New York, NY 10012.

ISBN: 978-0-545-13044-8

12 11 10 9 8 7 6 5 4 3   11 12 13 14 15/0

Printed in the U.S.A.
First printing, January 2010

CHAPTERS

I have a problem.

A really, really big problem.

My class is doing a penny drive

to raise money so we can adopt an

endangered species of penguin.

But I lost my penny collection.

Let me tell you about it.

CHAPTER 1

Penguins, Penguins, Penguins

"Okay, boys and girls," said my teacher, Mrs. Wushy, "now that we have read a lot about penguins, let's see if we can make a chart of some of the things we have learned."

"Oooooo, ooooooo, oooooo. I know!" Chloe squealed as she waved her hand wildly in the air.

"Hey, watch it!" Max snapped. "You're going to poke me in the eye."

"I am not," said Chloe.

"Yes you are, you little fancy-pants."

"Oh, no I'm not!"

"All right, enough, you two," said Mrs. Wushy. "Max, please come sit over here." She pointed to a place on the rug right next to her.

"But *she's* the one who almost hit *me*."

"Well, then this spot will be perfect for you. Chloe won't be able to reach you here, so you won't have to worry about being bumped by accident."

"But . . ."

"Max, I'm not asking you. I'm telling you," said Mrs. Wushy. "Let's go."

"It's not fair," Max mumbled under his breath, and then he slowly got up and moved over next to the teacher.

"Now, where were we?" asked Mrs. Wushy.

"You were asking us what we learned about penguins," said Jessie.

"Thank you, Jessie," said Mrs. Wushy.

Chloe waved her hand wildly again. "Oooooo, oooooo, oooooo!"

"Chloe, you need to raise your hand quietly and wait to be called on. I'm going to call on someone with a quiet hand."

Robbie, my best friend, who is a walking encyclopedia, was sitting quietly with his hand raised. "Robbie," said Mrs. Wushy, "what have you learned about penguins?"

"Penguins live in the Southern Hemisphere in places like Antarctica, South Africa, and New Zealand."

"Excellent, Robbie. You are absolutely right. Penguins live on the bottom half of the Earth."

Mrs. Wushy wrote Robbie's fact on the chart.

"You are such a brain," I whispered to Robbie. "I think you're the smartest person I know."

Robbie smiled. "Thanks."

Chloe was still *oooo, oooo, ooo*ing, so Mrs. Wushy called on Jessie next. "Jessie?"

"Penguins are really good swimmers, but they can't breathe underwater."

"That's right, Jessie. Penguins don't have gills like fish. They have lungs, so they have to come to the surface of the water to breathe air. I will write that on the chart."

Chloe had finally stopped squealing, so Mrs. Wushy called on her.

"Penguins eat fish, krill, or squid," Chloe said. "That sounds so disgusting to me. I'm glad I'm not a penguin." She twirled her curls around her finger.

"And remember," said Mrs. Wushy, "we read that they swallow their food whole."

"Cool," said Max. "I once tried to swallow a hot dog whole, but it didn't work."

"No kidding," Jessie whispered to me.

Mrs. Wushy ignored Max and continued. "Who else has a fact about penguins? How about you, Freddy?"

"Leopard seals eat penguins."

"Good. The leopard seal is the penguin's main predator. They are very big and have very sharp teeth. They have to eat about four to five penguins a day to stay alive."

"How sad," said Jessie. "How can they eat something so cute?"

"It's just part of the food chain," said Mrs. Wushy. "They are hungry, and they need to eat to stay warm.

"Let's see . . . who hasn't said anything yet? Max, how about you?"

"I . . . um . . . I . . . wasn't raising my hand."

"I know," said Mrs. Wushy, "but I'd like everyone to come up with something for the chart."

"Ummm . . . oh, I know!" he said. "Penguins lay eggs."

"Do you remember how many eggs a penguin lays at a time?"

"Ummm . . . uhhhh . . . I . . . ," Max stammered.

"Two eggs!" Chloe interrupted. "Penguins lay two eggs!"

"Be quiet!" yelled Max. "It's not your turn. It's my turn."

"But you didn't know the answer," Chloe said.

"Oh, yes I did!"

"No you didn't, or else you would have said it."

"Max and Chloe," said Mrs. Wushy, "you both need to stop this right now. No more arguing. Chloe, you interrupted Max, and that is not polite."

"Yeah," said Max.

"But he was taking forever," Chloe said.

"You had your turn," said Mrs. Wushy. "You need to let other people have their turns."

"I don't think she knows how to take turns," Jessie whispered to me.

"If you can't do that," Mrs. Wushy continued, "then you will have to sit in the time-out chair."

"Just put her there right now," Max mumbled.

"And, Max, you need to leave her alone, or else you will also get a visit to the time-out chair."

"Fine," Max said, shrugging.

Robbie raised his hand. "All penguins lay two eggs except the emperor and king penguins. They lay only one," he added.

"That is correct. Most penguins lay two eggs except for the ones that Robbie just mentioned."

"And . . . ," said Jessie.

"Yes?" said Mrs. Wushy.

"The mom and the dad take turns keeping the egg warm."

"Right. Since it is so cold where the penguins

live, the chick inside the egg would die if the egg was left uncovered for as little as five minutes, so the mom and dad can't leave the nest at the same time. If the mom goes to get food, then the dad sits on the eggs. When the mom comes back, then it's the dad's turn to look for food. Sometimes one of them can be gone for as long as two weeks!"

"Two weeks!" said Max. "I can't go without food for two *hours*."

"No kidding," I whispered to Robbie.

Robbie giggled.

"Penguins need to eat to stay warm. There is also something else that keeps them warm," said Mrs. Wushy. "Does anyone know what that is?"

Before anyone could answer, the bell rang for recess. "Oh my goodness! It's time for recess already. We will have to continue this when we come back inside."

CHAPTER 2

Playing Penguin

We all ran outside for recess. "Let's play penguin," said Jessie.

"That's a good idea," I said.

"I want to play," said Robbie.

"We can all play together," I said. "What should we do?"

"I know! I know!" said Jessie. "We can pretend that the play structure is an ice floe, and the sand is water. If you are in the sand, you'd better swim fast or else the leopard seals might eat you."

"And we can make a nest out of pebbles over there on the grass just like that one kind of penguin Mrs. Wushy was telling us about," I said.

"The Adélie penguins make their nests out of pebbles," said Robbie.

"Thanks, Super Scientist," I said, laughing.

"I think there are a bunch of pebbles over by those trees," said Jessie, pointing to a spot across the playground.

"Then let's go," I said. "What are we waiting for?" I started to run, but Jessie grabbed me.

"What?"

"Uh, hello! You're a penguin."

"I know."

"Well, penguins don't run. They waddle," said Jessie.

"Right!" I said, laughing.

We put our arms by our sides, and the three of us started to waddle across the playground.

As I was waddling across the yard, Max

ran right into me, sending me sailing to the pavement.

I hit the ground hard. "Oof!"

"Freddy, are you all right?" asked Robbie.

"Hey, Shark Breath, watch where you're going!" yelled Max.

"*He* ran into *me*," I said to Robbie.

"What did you say?" asked Max, bending down so that his face was close to mine. Talk about shark breath!

"Nothing," I said quietly.

"He said that you ran into him," said Jessie.

Boy, Jessie was so brave! She was the only one brave enough to stand up to Max, the biggest bully in the whole first grade.

"And I think that you should say you're sorry," she added.

Max stared at her for a minute and then started to walk away, but Jessie grabbed him.

"Take your hands off me!" shouted Max.

"Not until you tell Freddy you're sorry."

"It's okay," I said to Jessie.

"No, it's not. Max hurt you, and he needs to say he's sorry."

Max tried to squirm free, but Jessie held him tight. She was strong. "We're waiting," said Jessie, staring at Max.

"Sorry!" Max grunted, and then ran off.

"Are you okay?" Robbie asked.

"I think so," I said, pulling up my pant leg to look at my knee.

"I don't see any blood," said Robbie.

"I think I'll be okay," I said.

"Here, let me help you up," said Robbie.

I stood up and brushed myself off.

"Let's go, penguin friends," Jessie said, laughing. "Let's go get the pebbles for our nest."

We waddled over to the line of trees and started to pick up pebbles.

"Ooooh, look at this one," said Jessie. "It's so smooth and shiny."

"I found a bunch of good ones," I said, shoving them into my pocket.

"You know, the Adélie penguins use over one hundred pebbles to make their nests," said Robbie.

"One hundred! We'll never get that many!" I said.

"Well, we could start building it now, and

then work on it some more at lunch recess," said Jessie.

"Good idea," Robbie and I said.

We took the pebbles we had collected so far and carried them over to the grass. "Their nest is like a huge circle," said Robbie.

"The boy penguins usually make the nest while the girls go eat," said Jessie, "so I'm going to go catch some fish while you guys lay the pebbles out in a big circle."

"Don't get caught by the leopard seal!" I called after her.

"I won't!"

As Jessie ran over to the sandbox, Robbie and I started to lay the pebbles on the ground.

"How many do you think we have?" I asked Robbie.

"I don't know. Maybe twenty."

We started to count them, and then we heard Jessie yell, "Help me! Help! I'm being chased by a leopard seal."

"Don't worry! We'll save you!" Robbie and I yelled.

The two of us waddled over to the sandbox and started swimming as fast as we could. "Jump onto that ice floe! Jump onto that ice floe!" we shouted to Jessie.

Jessie jumped onto the play structure, and we followed her up there.

"Whew! That was a close one," said Jessie. "Thanks for saving me!"

"What are friends for?" I said, smiling. "Good thing you're a fast swimmer! That leopard seal looked really hungry."

"We'd better get back to building the nest, or it won't be ready for the eggs," said Robbie.

"Before we get back in the water, we'd better look for that leopard seal, or we might all get eaten!"

I looked over the edge of the play structure into the sand. "It looks like the coast is clear. Come on!"

We jumped into the water, swam to land, and then waddled back to the nest.

"We didn't get to put out all of the pebbles yet," said Robbie, "because we had to come save you."

"That's okay," said Jessie. "I'll help you with the rest."

We laid out the rest of the pebbles and then stood back to take a look.

"We are going to need a lot more," said Robbie.

"This is a big job," I said. "I wonder how the penguins do it. They must get really tired!"

"It is a lot of work," said Robbie. "And they have to do it every year."

"I didn't even know that there were rocks in Antarctica," said Jessie.

"Me either," I said. "I thought it was just a bunch of ice."

"It's volcanic rock," said Robbie. "It was formed a long time ago when volcanoes erupted there."

"Is there anything you don't know?" I said to Robbie.

He smiled.

"Come on, guys," said Jessie. "Recess is almost—"

Before she could say the word *over*, the bell rang, signaling the end of recess.

"Bummer," I said. "I was having so much fun."

"Me, too," said Robbie.

"Don't worry, guys. We can play again at lunch recess," said Jessie. "Now we'd better hurry up, or we'll be late getting into line."

"Last one there is a rotten egg!" I yelled as I took off waddling across the playground.

CHAPTER 3

Blubber

When we got back into class, Mrs. Wushy said, "Right before you went out to recess, I asked if anyone knew how penguins stay warm."

"I think I know," said Robbie. "One time I read in a book that penguins have a layer of blubber under their skin."

"That's right, Robbie."

"Blubber? What's blubber?" Max yelled out.

"Max, please don't call out," said Mrs. Wushy.

"Blubber, blubber, blubber," sang Max.

Mrs. Wushy stared at him, and he got quiet. I guess he didn't want a trip to the time-out chair.

"Blubber is a layer of fat," Mrs. Wushy said.

"Eeeewwww!" said Chloe, wrinkling up her nose. "That is disgusting!"

"No, it's not," said Mrs. Wushy. "If the penguins didn't have the blubber, then they might freeze to death. That extra layer of fat helps keep them alive. They also have two more layers that keep them warm."

"Really?" said Jessie.

"Really. They have a layer of feathers right next to their skin. All of those feathers are down feathers."

"My nana bought me a down comforter for my bed," said Chloe, "and it keeps me toasty warm in the winter."

"Well, just like the down feathers in your comforter keep you warm, the down feathers on the penguin keep it warm during the long, cold winters."

"Cool! It's like it has its own down comforter," I said, laughing.

"I guess you could say that," said Mrs. Wushy, smiling.

"But that's only two layers," said Jessie. "What's the third one?"

"There is a top layer of feathers on a penguin, and these are tightly packed together, and they are waterproof."

"Sort of like a wet suit?" asked Robbie.

"Exactly," said Mrs. Wushy. "That top layer of feathers is covered with a special oil that keeps the penguin dry. When he goes swimming in the freezing water, it can't soak down into his skin. It just rolls off his back."

Mrs. Wushy drew a picture of the three layers on the board. "Would you all like to do an experiment that shows how the blubber keeps the penguin warm?"

BLUBBER

DOWN FEATHERS

TOP LAYER

"Yes!" we all said excitedly.

"I'm going to need a volunteer."

"Ooooo, ooooo, oooo! Me! Me! Me!" Chloe squealed.

"Mrs. Wushy is not going to pick her," Jessie whispered to me.

"Remember, Chloe," said Mrs. Wushy, "I only pick quiet people."

Jessie and I smiled at each other.

"Let's see. Who has been a good listener all morning? Robbie, would you like to help me with this experiment?"

"Sure!" said Robbie.

"That's not fair!" said Max.

"Yes it is," said Mrs. Wushy. "Robbie has been on his best behavior all morning. If you want to be picked to do things, then you need to be a better listener.

"Now," said Mrs. Wushy, "we are going to compare what it is like to put your hand in ice water if you have blubber with what it is like if you don't have blubber."

"But I don't have blubber," said Robbie, laughing.

"We are going to pretend like you do," said Mrs. Wushy. "First, I am going to put your left hand in this plastic bag and tape it closed so no water can get in. Then I am going to cover your right hand in this cooking fat called shortening that is exactly like the blubber on a penguin, and then put that hand in a plastic bag and tape it closed."

"Cool!" said Max.

After she put the bags on Robbie's hands, Mrs. Wushy said, "Robbie, you are going to put both hands into this bucket of ice water, and we are going to see how long you can keep your hands in the water before they get too cold."

Robbie held up his hands in the bags, and we all laughed.

"Are you ready?"

"Yes!"

"Then when I say go, put both hands in the water at the same time. Okay?" said Mrs. Wushy.

"Okeydokey!" said Robbie.

"Ready, set, go!"

Robbie shoved both of his hands into the bucket of water. "Wow! This water is really cold."

"Keep your hands in there for as long as you can," said Mrs. Wushy. "I'm timing you."

After only about ten seconds, Robbie had to pull his left hand out of the water. "My fingers on this hand feel like Popsicles!" he said.

"Grape or cherry?" said Chloe.

"Can I lick them?" Max asked, chuckling.

"Uh, no!" said Robbie. "That's gross."

After about ten more seconds, Robbie pulled his right hand out of the water. "That's amazing!" he said. "The blubber kept this hand a lot warmer."

"You were able to keep your blubber-covered hand in the water for twice as long," said Mrs. Wushy. "So you can see how having that layer of blubber under their skin really helps the penguins survive in their freezing environment."

"I'll rub a bunch of that stuff all over my body so I can go swimming in the winter!" Max said.

"Or you could just wear a wet suit," said Robbie. "It would keep you warm, and you wouldn't look like a giant grease ball."

"A giant grease ball." I giggled. "That's a good one."

"Thank you, Robbie," said Mrs. Wushy. "You were a great volunteer."

"Can I be next? Can I be next?" Chloe whined.

"I'm sorry, Chloe. We're not going to do the experiment again today, but you can try it at home with your family if you'd like. You just need to get small plastic bags, tape, some shortening, and a bucket of ice water."

"But my mom never lets me do anything messy," said Chloe, pouting. "She doesn't want me to ruin my beautiful dresses and my shiny nail polish."

"Oh, brother," Jessie whispered.

"Robbie," said Mrs. Wushy, "why don't you go

wash off your hands? It's almost time for lunch, and I don't think you want to eat grease."

While Mrs. Wushy cleaned up, Robbie washed off his hands and then sat down.

"I love learning about penguins," said Jessie. "I always thought they were cute, but now I know lots of interesting things about them. Someday I want to go see them in person."

"Let's hope that they will still be here when you are older," said Mrs. Wushy.

"What do you mean?" asked Jessie.

"I'll explain it to you after lunch. Right now it's time for you little penguins to go eat some fish sticks in the cafeteria."

CHAPTER 4

Endangered Animals

We had fun playing penguin again at lunch recess. We almost finished building our nest. I think we were up to seventy-five pebbles.

When we got back to the classroom, Jessie asked, "Mrs. Wushy, can you tell me what you meant when you said, 'Let's hope they will still be here when you are older'?"

"Sure," said Mrs. Wushy. "Some animals are becoming endangered. Do you know what that means?"

"Not really."

"It means that for different reasons many of them are dying, and if we humans don't do something to protect them, then they will become extinct. Who knows what 'extinct' means?"

"It means that there won't be any more left on the planet," said Robbie.

"Like the dinosaurs?" said Max.

"Yes, like the dinosaurs," said Mrs. Wushy.

"Are all penguins endangered?" asked Robbie.

"Not all penguins, but the Galápagos penguins that live on the Galápagos Islands off the coast of South America are."

"But why are the penguins dying?" asked Jessie.

"Mostly because the Earth is getting warmer and warmer, so the penguins' habitat is shrinking."

"Why is the Earth getting warmer?" I asked.

41

"It's sort of complicated," said Mrs. Wushy, "but we humans are to blame. You see, the sun has warmed our planet for millions of years. But right now, our cars and factories are making a lot of pollution that goes up into the air and traps the sun's heat. A long time ago, the sun's heat could escape, but now more and more of it is getting trapped, and the planet is getting hotter and hotter."

"That can't be good," said Robbie.

"It's not," said Mrs. Wushy. "And penguins are not the only animals that are being affected. There are a lot of animals in danger."

"I don't want to think of what the Earth would be like without animals," said Jessie.

"Me neither," I said.

"That's why it's important for humans to do things to protect the animals and their habitats."

"But what can we do?"

"My mom knows a lot about this stuff," said Robbie, "because she works at the natural history museum. One time she told me about an organization that works really hard to protect endangered animals. She said that you can actually adopt an endangered animal to help keep it safe."

"Can we adopt a penguin?" asked Chloe. "Can we? Can we? It could be our class pet!"

"You can't bring it here to the classroom, Ding-Dong," said Max.

"Why not?"

"Because it's not cold enough here. It would die."

"But we could keep it in a tub of ice water," said Chloe, "and feed it fish sticks."

"Is she for real?" Jessie whispered.

Robbie just rolled his eyes.

"We can't keep a penguin in our classroom,

Chloe," said Mrs. Wushy. "Besides, when you adopt a wild animal, it doesn't really mean that you bring it home with you."

"It doesn't?"

"No, it means that you are donating money to help protect it and its environment."

"That still sounds like a cool idea," said Robbie. "Can we do it?"

"I've adopted animals with my classes before," said Mrs. Wushy. "It costs about twenty dollars."

"Where did you get the money?" asked Jessie.

"We had to raise it."

"How did you do that?" I asked.

"We decided as a class what we wanted to do to raise money. Then we went out and did it."

"Can we do it? Can we do it?" we all asked.

"Of course we can do it," said Mrs. Wushy. "We just have to come up with an idea for raising the money."

Kids started shouting out ideas.

"Hold on, everyone," said Mrs. Wushy. "I can't hear when you are all shouting at once. I have a better idea. Why don't you all go home tonight and talk about it with your parents? Brainstorm some ideas for raising money, and then bring your ideas to school tomorrow."

"But what if we have lots of different ideas?" asked Jessie. "How will we choose one?"

"You'll choose my idea," said Chloe, "because I am going to come up with the best one."

"Says who?" said Max.

"Me, that's who!" Chloe snapped back.

"Well, you're wrong. Mine is going to be the best," said Max.

"Stop it, you two," said Mrs. Wushy. "We will choose an idea the fair way. We will vote on it."

"That sounds fair," said Robbie.

"So go home tonight and talk about it with your families," said Mrs. Wushy. "Bring your ideas to school tomorrow, and we will vote. The idea that gets the most votes will be the one that we do."

"I can't wait to talk to Suzie," I said to Robbie.

"Really? Usually you think she's annoying."

"Yeah. Usually I do, but I know she did this when she was in Mrs. Wushy's class, and I think they raised a lot of money. I bet she has some good ideas."

"Can you share some of them with me?" Robbie asked.

"No way!" I said. "Besides, I'm sure your mom has a gazillion ideas. I bet one of your ideas gets picked."

"I guess we'll see tomorrow," said Robbie.

"Yep, we'll see tomorrow," I said, smiling.

CHAPTER 5

Ideas, Anyone?

"Hey, guess what?" I said that night at dinner.

"You're going to live with Robbie from now on?" Suzie said.

"Ha-ha, very funny. No, I'm not moving out."

"It was worth a try," Suzie mumbled under her breath.

"Suzie," said my mom, "be nice to your brother."

"We're learning about penguins at school,"

I said. "And do you want to know something funny?"

"Sure," said my dad.

"We're eating macaroni tonight, and there's a penguin named the macaroni penguin!"

"Really?" said my mom.

"Yep!"

"I've never heard of a macaroni penguin," said my mom. "I've only heard of emperor penguins."

"The emperor is the most famous," I said, "but there are actually about seventeen species of penguins in the world."

"I never knew that."

"They all live on the bottom half of the Earth."

"But I thought they lived where the polar bears were," said my mom, "and the polar bears live at the top of the Earth in the Arctic."

"A lot of people think that," I said, "but there are no penguins in the Arctic. If polar bears and

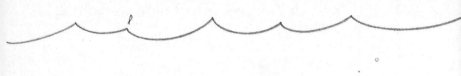

penguins lived in the same place, then the bears might eat the penguins!"

"How could you eat something so cute?" said Suzie.

"Penguins can't fly, but they are really good swimmers. They use their wings like paddles."

"How do they breathe underwater?" asked my mom.

"They have to hold their breath underwater, like humans, and then they have to come up for air. They can usually stay underwater for

about three minutes before they have to come up."

"You sure do know a lot about penguins," said my dad.

"I can tell you more," I said. "Did you know that some of the penguins in the world are endangered?"

"I didn't know that penguins were on the endangered species list," said my dad.

"Well, they are," I said. "My class decided to adopt a penguin to help protect it."

"What a wonderful idea," said my mom.

"Didn't you do something like that when you were in Mrs. Wushy's class?" my dad asked Suzie.

"Yes, but we didn't adopt a penguin. We adopted a gorilla because we were learning about Africa."

"Well, I think it's a great idea," said my mom. "I wouldn't want to imagine what the world would be like if we didn't have animals."

I put some macaroni on my head, and then I jumped out of my chair and started waddling around the kitchen table.

"Freddy," said my mom, "what are you doing? You're supposed to be eating your dinner, not wearing it."

I ignored her and waddled over to Suzie.

"Get out of here, Weirdo," Suzie said, giving me a little shove.

I lost my balance and bumped into the kitchen table, spilling my glass of milk.

"Oh my goodness! Now look what you've done, Freddy!" my mom said.

"What *I've* done? Suzie pushed me into the table!"

"But if you were sitting down like you are supposed to, then this wouldn't have happened," my mom said, running over to the sink to grab a sponge and some paper towels.

I glared at Suzie, and she stuck her tongue out at me.

My mom came back and wiped up the milk. "Now, Freddy, sit down so I can get the macaroni out of your hair!"

"But I'm a macaroni penguin," I said, laughing.

"Look at this mess!" said my mom. "It's all stuck in your hair. You're going to have to take a shower tonight."

"No! I did last night."

"Too bad. You're not going to school tomorrow with macaroni in your hair. Now sit still until dinner is over. I don't want any more accidents."

I sat down. "Tomorrow I'm supposed to bring in some ideas for how we can raise money to adopt the penguin."

"How much does it cost?" asked my dad.

"About twenty dollars."

"That shouldn't be too hard to raise," said my mom. "How about a bake sale?"

"Nah. Everybody does bake sales. We are going to vote on the ideas tomorrow, and I bet a bunch of people bring in that idea. I want to think of something different."

"What about a car wash?" my dad suggested.

"The kids in my class are too small for that," I said. "We wouldn't be able to reach the top of the cars."

"That's probably true," my dad said, chuckling.

"How about selling raffle tickets?" said my mom.

102605

"I thought about that," I said, "but we don't have a prize to raffle off."

"Collecting bottles and cans?" said my dad.

"That's not a bad one," I said. "I could maybe suggest that tomorrow."

"Excuse me," said Suzie, "but I have to go do my homework."

"You may be excused," said my mom and dad.

Suzie cleared her plate and left the room.

"Uh, may I please be excused?" I asked.

"But I thought you wanted to think of some more ideas for tomorrow," said my mom.

"Right now I have to go take a shower," I said as I raced up the stairs.

I ran into Suzie's room.

"Get out of my room!" she yelled. "I'm trying to do my homework."

"I just need an idea."

"Go ask Mom and Dad."

"No, I want *you* to give me an idea."

"For what?"

"To raise money for the penguin adoption. I
want to know what you did with your class."

"What's it worth to you?" Suzie asked, holding
up her pinkie for a pinkie swear.

"Ummm . . . ummm."

"Let's go. I haven't got all night."

"You get to shower first tonight."

"Just tonight? It's three nights or no deal!"

"Three nights!"

"Do we have a deal?"

I really wanted her idea, because I just knew it would be a good one. "Deal," I said as we locked pinkies. "Now tell me your idea."

"A penny drive," Suzie said, smiling.

"A penny drive?"

"Yep. You can call it Pennies for Penguins. You just ask everybody to bring in their pennies. Most people have a bunch just sitting around in a jar like we do. You'd be surprised how quickly they add up."

"That's a great idea!" I said. "Thanks! You're the best sister in the whole world!"

"I know," Suzie said, smiling. "Now get out of my room so I can finish my homework."

CHAPTER 6

The Vote

The next day at school we were all excited about our ideas.

"Did you talk to Suzie last night?" Robbie asked.

"Yes, I did," I said, smiling. "She gave me a great idea. How about you? Did you talk to your mom?"

"Yep," said Robbie. "I think my idea is pretty good."

"I have the best idea," Chloe interrupted. "Everyone's going to want to do mine."

"No way!" said Max. "I'm sure your idea is really lame."

"It is not!" Chloe whined.

"All right, everybody," said Mrs. Wushy. "Come on over to the rug so we can all hear your great ideas."

We sat down, and Mrs. Wushy took out a big

piece of paper. "I am going to write all of your ideas down on this piece of paper, and then we will vote. I want everyone to respect what people say. You are not allowed to make fun of anyone's ideas."

"But what if the idea is really dumb?" said Max.

"There is no such thing as a dumb idea," said Mrs. Wushy. "If you can't say something nice, then don't say anything at all."

"Does he ever say anything nice?" I whispered to Robbie.

He shook his head.

"Who would like to go first?" asked Mrs. Wushy.

I didn't want to go first, because I wanted to save the best for last, so I waited to put my hand up. Of course, Chloe was waving her hand around so hard that I thought it was going to break off.

"Chloe," said Mrs. Wushy, "since you are

not calling out, would you like to go first?"

"Yes, I would," she said as she stood up and walked to the front of the room.

"You can just tell us from your seat if you'd like," said Mrs. Wushy.

"No, I want to come up here," said Chloe. "It's such a good idea that I want to see everyone's faces when I say it."

"Oh boy, here we go," whispered Jessie.

"Uhh, hmmm," Chloe said, clearing her throat. "I think we should set up the classroom like a beauty salon, and kids can come here to get their fingernails painted with polish. We can have all kinds of pretty colors to choose from, and they can pay us two dollars to get their nails done."

"Is she kidding?" Robbie whispered to me.

"Oh no. She's serious."

"That is the dumbest idea I ever heard!" shouted Max. "No boy is going to want to get his nails painted."

"Max," said Mrs. Wushy, "what did I say about telling other children their ideas are dumb?"

"You said I couldn't say that."

"That's right, so you need to apologize to Chloe."

"But . . . but . . ."

"Apologize right now, or you will be taking a trip to the time-out chair and you won't get to vote."

Max looked at Mrs. Wushy for a minute, and I guess then he decided that it was too early in the morning for the time-out chair, so he mumbled, "I'm sorry."

Mrs. Wushy turned back to Chloe. "Thank you for your idea. I will write it on our chart, and you can go back and sit down."

Chloe's lip dropped into a pout, and she walked back to sit down.

"Who would like to go next?"

Robbie raised his hand.

"Yes, Robbie."

"I think we should have a big jar filled with jelly beans, and kids have to pay twenty-five cents to guess how many jelly beans are in the jar. The person who has the closest guess wins the jar of candy."

There were a lot of oohs and aahs from the class. Robbie smiled.

"You're right. That *is* a good idea," I said.

"I'll add it to the list," said Mrs. Wushy.

"I have an idea," said Jessie. "We can sell Popsicles at snack time. We can call it Popsicles for the Penguins."

Mrs. Wushy wrote "Popsicle sale" on the chart.

A few other kids made suggestions. The usual: bake sale, bottle drive, car wash. Then I raised my hand.

"Yes, Freddy," said Mrs. Wushy. "Do you have an idea?"

"I sure do. A penny drive," I said. "We can call it Pennies for Penguins."

"Another great idea," said Mrs. Wushy, adding it to the chart.

"Good one," Jessie whispered.

"I think we are just about ready to vote, unless anyone else has something to add."

None of the other kids raised their hands.

"Okay, then," said Mrs. Wushy. "I want this to be a fair vote, so I'm going to ask you to close your eyes. Raise your hand when you hear me read your choice. Please remember that you can only vote once, so make sure you know exactly which one you are going to choose."

Mrs. Wushy read all the suggestions one more time so we would know which one we wanted to vote for.

"I think we are ready now, so, everyone, please close your eyes."

"But Max is peeking," Chloe whined.

"The only way you would know that Max was peeking is if you also had your eyes open," said Mrs. Wushy. "So the two of you both need to keep your eyes closed or else you will not be allowed to vote. Understand?"

They both nodded. "I will say it one more time. Everyone please close your eyes."

We all closed our eyes, and Mrs. Wushy read

each idea for us to vote on. When she got to the end of the list, she paused a minute and then said, "You can all open your eyes now."

My heart was beating fast. "I hope my idea wins," I whispered to Jessie.

"Well, it looks like we have a tie," said Mrs. Wushy. "We will have to have another vote."

"I just know my idea is part of the tie," Chloe boasted.

"Actually, it's not," said Mrs. Wushy.

"There's a surprise," Jessie whispered.

"The tie is between Freddy and Robbie."

We both looked at each other and giggled. "I can't believe it," I said.

"Me either," said Robbie.

"We are going to vote one more time," said Mrs. Wushy. "Your choice is a penny drive or the jelly bean guessing jar. Everyone ready? Okay, close your eyes."

"Good luck," I whispered to Robbie.

"Yeah. Good luck," he whispered back.

We voted again, and Mrs. Wushy said, "You all can open your eyes now. We have a winner."

Now my heart was beating so fast I thought it was going to pop out of my chest. I looked at Robbie.

Robbie looked at me.

"The winning idea is the penny drive. Congratulations, Freddy. That was a great idea you brought in. So now everybody needs to go home tonight, find some pennies, and bring them in!"

CHAPTER 7

Penny Problems

When I got home from school, I went running into the kitchen. "Mom! Mom! Guess what!" I yelled as I jumped up and down. "Guess what!"

Suzie was there having her snack. "Calm down. You look like a monkey, jumping around like that."

"What, Freddy?" said my mom. "What are you so excited about?"

"The class picked my idea!"

"That's wonderful, honey, but I have no idea what you're talking about."

"The class picked my idea for raising money for the penguin adoption."

"I knew they would like the idea of collecting bottles and cans."

"No, no, no! Not that!" I said. "A penny drive."

"A penny drive? That's a great idea!" said my mom.

"Yes, it is," Suzie said, smiling.

"Well, the class really liked my idea and Robbie's idea. When we took a vote, it was a tie, so we took another vote, and my idea won!"

"Well, that's great, Freddy. I am so happy for you."

"Thanks, Mom," I said.

Suzie just gave me a look.

"So, Freddy," said my mom, "are you hungry? Do you want a snack?"

"No thanks! I'm going to find my penny jar.

Mrs. Wushy said that we need to bring in two thousand pennies if we want to raise twenty dollars."

"That sure is a lot of pennies!" said my mom.

"I know it. But since there are twenty kids in our class, if everyone brings in one hundred pennies, then we will have enough."

"Are you sure you don't want even a little something to eat?" my mom asked.

"No thanks!" I called over my shoulder as I ran out of the kitchen and up the stairs. "I've got to find those pennies!"

I ran into my room and yanked open the bottom drawer of my desk. To my surprise, my penny jar wasn't there. I sat down on the edge of my bed and hit my forehead with the palm of my hand.

"Think, think, think."

Now, where could that jar be? I thought for sure I had put it in my desk drawer.

I ran over to my closet and threw open the

door. My baseball bat tumbled onto my bedroom floor, and a basketball rolled halfway across the room. As I stepped partway inside, I tripped on my sharkhead flashlight. I always shove things into my closet, because my mom is a neat freak, and she gets upset if my room isn't clean. I just have to hope that she doesn't ever open that door!

I picked up the flashlight, turned it on, and shined it around the dark inside of the closet. "That penny jar has got to be in here somewhere," I mumbled.

I lifted my suitcase. Not there. I shoved aside a blow-up shark I had won at the carnival. Not there. I checked behind my box of Commander Upchuck action figures. Not there!

I put the flashlight down and started tossing things out of my closet. "It's got to be here somewhere!" I said to myself.

Eventually everything that had been in my closet was all over my bedroom floor, and I still hadn't found the penny jar.

I was starting to panic. I just had to find those pennies!

"Oh, I know!" I said to myself. "I must have hidden it in my underwear drawer." I put things in there when I don't want Suzie to find them. She thinks my underwear is gross, so she never opens that drawer.

I made my way through the maze of toys that was now all over my floor, and I pulled open my underwear drawer. I was tossing my underwear out of the drawer when Suzie walked into the room. A pair of underwear hit her in the face.

"Eeewww! Eeewww!" she screamed. "That is disgusting! You just threw a pair of underwear in my face!"

"Maybe that will teach you not to walk into my room without knocking first," I said.

"What are you doing in here, anyway? Mom is going to freak out when she sees this mess!"

"I'm trying to find my penny jar. You must have taken it, because I can't find it anywhere!"

"Taken it? Why would I take it?"

"Because you always take my stuff without asking."

"No I don't!"

"Yes you do."

"Oh, no I don't!"

"Oh, yes you do!"

Just then my mom came up the stairs. "What is going on in . . . ?" She stopped in the middle of her sentence when she got to the door of my room. "Freddy! Look at this mess! What are you doing?"

"I think you should punish him, Mom," said Suzie. "Look what he did to his room."

I glared at Suzie.

"Suzie, you need to stay out of this," said my mom. "I'm talking to Freddy right now. I'm going to ask you again, Freddy. What are you doing?"

I sniffled a little bit, and then I started to cry. "I'm . . . I'm . . . I'm sorry, Mom. I . . . I . . . I was just trying to find my penny jar. I have to bring in one hundred pennies tomorrow. I know . . . I have . . . one hundred pennies in my penny jar . . . but I can't find it!" I sobbed.

"Calm down, Freddy," said my mom. "It's not the end of the world. If we can't find the

jar, you can always just bring in a dollar. A dollar is worth one hundred pennies."

"No I can't!" I cried. "It's not called Dollars for Penguins. It's called Pennies for Penguins. Now we won't be able to adopt the penguin, and it will all be my fault."

"All right, all right," said my mom. "We'll find your penny jar. Don't worry."

"Thanks, Mom," I sniffled.

"Now, let's think. Where do you remember seeing it last?"

"I thought it was in my desk drawer, but it wasn't there, so I looked in my closet, and it wasn't there, either."

"I can see that," said my mom, looking around at the mess in my room.

"The last place I looked was in my underwear drawer, but it wasn't there, either."

"Hmmm. It is a mystery."

Just then Suzie bolted out of the room.

"Suzie, where are you going?" yelled my mom.

"I'll be back in a minute!" she called as she ran down the stairs. We heard the back door open.

Two minutes later, Suzie was back in my room, holding my penny jar in her hands and smiling.

"Where did you find it? Where did you find it?" I said, jumping up and down excitedly.

"In the tree house."

"In the tree house?" I said. "How'd it get there?"

"You and Robbie must have taken it up to the tree house the last time he was over," said Suzie. "I remembered seeing it when Kimberly and I went up there to play after school yesterday."

"Thank you! Thank you! Thank you!" I said, giving Suzie a big hug.

"You are a great detective, Suzie," said my mom. "Thanks for solving the mystery."

Suzie smiled.

"Now let's get out of here so your brother can clean up this mess!"

CHAPTER 8

Pennies for Penguins

I ran into school the next day with my jar full of pennies. I couldn't wait to see if the class had collected enough.

"Do you have your pennies?" Robbie asked.

"Yep. Right here," I said, holding up the jar.

"I meant to remind you that we had taken them up to the tree house the last time I was over at your house."

"Yeah, thanks a lot," I said. "I tore my whole

room apart yesterday looking for them. It looked like a tornado hit my room."

"Your mom must have loved that!" Robbie chuckled.

"It took me over an hour just to get everything put away!"

"Well, I'm just glad you found the jar."

"Actually, Suzie found it."

"You owe her one," said Robbie.

"I know, but you don't need to remind her," I said, laughing.

"Okay, everyone," said Mrs. Wushy. "Bring your pennies over to the rug. We need to start counting."

We all carried our pennies to the rug.

"My pennies are all shiny and new," Chloe bragged.

"So what?" said Max.

"So they look really pretty."

"That doesn't matter," said Max. "The pennies don't have to be pretty."

"That's right," said Mrs. Wushy. "But we do need to count them to make sure we have two thousand."

"That's a lot of counting," said Jessie.

"Yes, it is, but if we cooperate and work together, then it will be easy to count them all," said Mrs. Wushy. "I know you can do it."

We nodded.

"This is what you are going to do," said Mrs. Wushy. "You are going to count your pennies out into piles of ten. Does anyone remember how many groups of ten make one hundred?"

"Ten!" we yelled out.

"You are all so smart!" said Mrs. Wushy, smiling. "That's right. Ten groups of ten make one hundred. You can start counting now."

We all dumped our pennies out onto the floor and started stacking them up into piles of ten.

"I'm done counting!" shouted Chloe. "I'm the first one done!"

"Whoop-de-doo for you!" Jessie whispered to me.

I giggled.

"No you're not!" shouted Max. "I was the first one done!"

"No, I was!" yelled Chloe.

"No way, fancy-pants!" said Max.

"You two need to stop fighting," said Mrs.

Wushy. "Remember, we are working together as a class. It doesn't matter who was done first."

Mrs. Wushy glanced around the room. "It looks like everyone is done now."

We all nodded.

"Great! Does everyone have one hundred pennies?"

Just then a boy named Ryan started to cry.

"What's wrong, Ryan?" asked Mrs. Wushy. "Why are you crying?"

"I . . . I . . . I know I had one hundred pennies in my bag this morning, but . . . but . . . but now I only have ninety-eight!"

"Great! Just great!" said Max. "Now we don't have enough money."

Ryan started crying even louder. "Waaaahhhh!"

"Don't worry, Ryan," I said, standing up and walking over to him. "I brought some extra pennies just in case." I reached deep down into my pocket and pulled out two pennies. "Here you go!" I said, handing them to him.

"Thank you, Freddy," he said, sniffling.

"Yes, thank you, Freddy," said Mrs. Wushy. "What a nice friend you are."

I smiled.

"Now, let's check again," said Mrs. Wushy. "Does everyone have one hundred pennies?"

"I do! I do!" we all said.

"Great!" said Mrs. Wushy. "If we have twenty kids in our class, and they each have one hundred pennies, then we have two thousand pennies in total. That makes twenty dollars, enough to adopt a penguin."

"Hooray!" we all cheered. "Hooray!"

"I will collect all of our money and send it off to the animal defenders organization today," said Mrs. Wushy. "In a few weeks, they will send us a special certificate and a picture of our new baby."

"I can't wait!" said Jessie. "It's going to be so cute!"

"I am so proud of all of you!" said Mrs. Wushy. "Thank you for caring about our planet and the animals we share it with."

Robbie, Jessie, and I started waddling around the room.

"What are you weirdos doing?" said Max.

"It's a penguin party!" Jessie said. "Come on!"

Soon everyone else joined in, waddling and giggling and laughing . . . even Max.

DEAR READER,

I love animals! I have four dogs that I adopted from our local animal shelter. They are all very special to me, and I can't imagine living without them.

There are so many beautiful animals on our planet. We need to make sure that we do all we can to protect them. If we don't, then many more animals will become extinct.

Would you like to help protect an animal by adopting it, just like Freddy's class did? Here are two organizations that have animal adoption programs:

National Wildlife Federation (www.nwf.org)
Defenders of Wildlife (www.defenders.org)

Have you ever adopted an animal or joined an organization that protects animals? I would love to hear about it. Just write to me at:

Ready, Freddy! Fun Stuff
c/o Scholastic Inc.
P.O. Box 711
New York, NY 10013-0711

I hope you had as much fun reading *The Penguin Problem* as I had writing it.

HAPPY READING!

Abby Klein

Freddy's Fun Pages

FREDDY'S SHARK JOURNAL

GREENLAND SHARKS

Penguins live in freezing water. Is there a shark that can survive living in water that cold? Yes! The Greenland shark!

Greenland sharks live in the cold waters of the North Atlantic Ocean near Greenland and Iceland.

Greenland sharks are very large. They can be as big as a great white shark.

Greenland sharks eat fish and seals.

The flesh of the Greenland shark is poisonous if you eat it fresh.

Greenland sharks are not dangerous to humans.

PENGUIN QUIZ: TRUE OR FALSE?

Are you a penguin expert?
Take this penguin quiz to find out!

1. Penguins are mammals.

2. Penguins live only in the Southern Hemisphere.

3. Some penguins can fly.

4. A penguin colony is called a herd.

5. Penguins lay eggs.

6. Penguins swallow their food whole.

1. False—they are birds. 2. True 3. False—they can only walk and swim. 4. False—it is called a rookery. 5. True 6. True

WHO AM I?

There are many different species of penguins. Do you know what kind of penguin I am?

1. I am the largest species of penguin

2. I build my nest out of stones.

3. I have yellow and black feathers sticking out the sides of my head.

4. My nickname is the blackfoot penguin.

CHOICES:

macaroni   Adélie

African   emperor

1. emperor 2. Adélie 3. macaroni 4. African

PENGUIN FUN

You and your friends can make a
penguin using your hands and feet!
Just follow these simple directions.

YOU WILL NEED:

> **black, white, and orange construction paper**
> **pencil**
> **scissors**
> **glue**
> **two googly eyes**

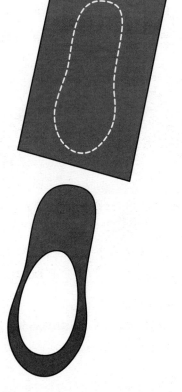

1. Trace around one
of your shoes on the
black construction
paper. Cut it out. This
is your head and body.

2. Cut an oval for
the belly out of the
white construction
paper. Glue it on top
of your black piece.

3. Fold a piece of black construction paper in half. Squeeze your fingers together and trace around your hand on the black paper. Leave the paper folded and cut out your hand shape. You now have two wings. Glue them to the side of the body.

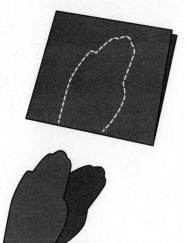

4. Glue two googly eyes onto the face.

5. Cut out an orange triangle for the beak. Glue it under the eyes.

6. Cut a 2-inch circle out of orange construction paper. Cut the circle in half to make two feet. Glue the feet to the bottom of the body.

You did it!
Now you can hang your penguin up in your room or use it to decorate your classroom.

Have you read all about Freddy?

Don't miss any of Freddy's funny adventures!